DC COMICS™
SUPER HEROES

WONDER WOMAN™

AN ORIGIN STORY

STONE ARCH BOOKS
A CAPSTONE IMPRINT

Published by Stone Arch Books in 2015
A Capstone Imprint
1710 Roe Crest Drive
North Mankato, MN 56003
www.capstonepub.com

STAR34386

Cataloging-in-Publication Data is available at the Library of Congress website
ISBN: 978-1-4342-9729-7 (library binding)
ISBN: 978-1-4342-9733-4 (paperback)
ISBN: 978-1-4965-0163-9 (eBook)

Summary: She was once a young princess on the secret island inhabited by warrior women known as the
Amazons...but she left her homeland--and her royal birthright--behind to become a protector for the entire
planet of Earth: Wonder Woman! Follow young Diana's incredible transformation from princess to super hero
in this action-packed chapter book for early readers featuring colorful illustrations by DC Comics artists.

Contributing artists: Dan Schoening and Ethen Beavers
Designed by Hilary Wacholz

Printed in the United States of America in North Mankato, Minnesota
122019   000113

WONDER WOMAN

AN ORIGIN STORY

WRITTEN BY
JOHN SAZAKALIS

ILLUSTRATED BY
LUCIANO VECCHIO

WONDER WOMAN CREATED BY
WILLIAM MOULTON MARSTON

Welcome to the beautiful island of Themyscira. It is surrounded by crystal-clear water. It is full of lush, green plant life. But Themyscira can't be seen on any map!

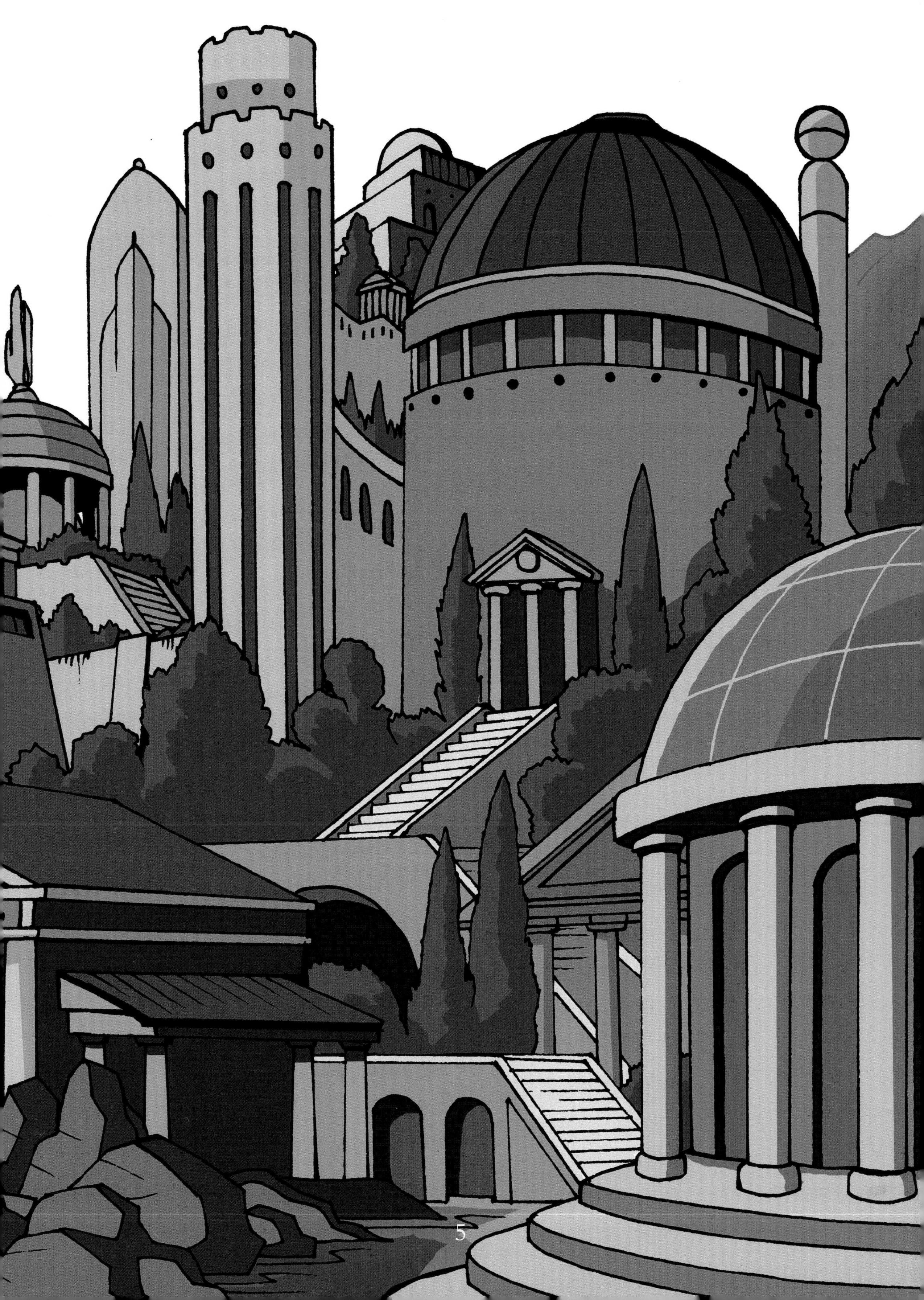

This secret place is the home of the Amazons. They are a tribe of female warriors. They are all experts in combat. Their queen, Hippolyta, leads them. She is a fair ruler.

Hippolyta's daughter is the princess. Her name is Diana. She is the heir to the throne. Diana is confident. She is determined. She has a heart of gold.

When she was born, Diana was
given many gifts from the Greek gods.

Zeus is the king of the Greek gods. This lord of lightning gave Diana the gift of strength.

Hermes is the swift-footed messenger. He gave her the gift of speed.

Aphrodite is the goddess of love. She gave Diana the gift of beauty.

Athena is intelligent and wise. She gave Diana the gift of wisdom.

From a young age, Diana was
taught her royal duties. She learned
the proper etiquette of a princess.
She also loved to be outdoors. She
enjoyed playing games with all of
her friends.

Whenever the queen was busy, Diana would leave the palace. She climbed trees in the forests. She ran through the meadows. She dived off cliffs into the sea.

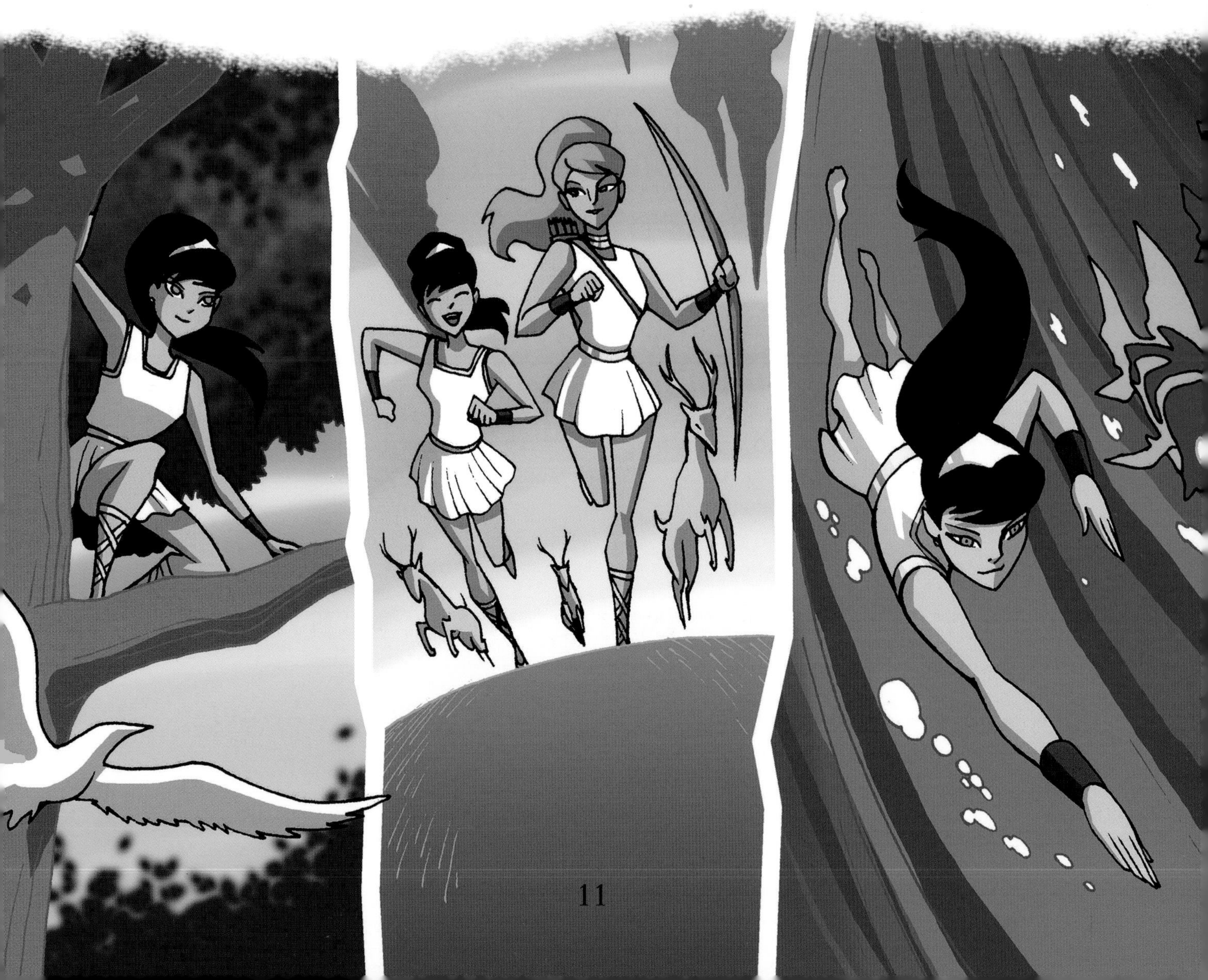

When Diana grew older, Hippolyta showed her a glimpse of the world beyond Themyscira. The princess saw the many evils that harmed it.

"What is happening?" Diana asked.

"The rest of the world does not live in peace and harmony. Ares, the god of war, causes pain and violence," her mother explained.

"They are suffering," the princess said. "We must help them!"

The queen agreed that something must be done.

The next day, Queen Hippolyta spoke to all of the Amazons.

"We will send an ambassador of peace to aid the world of man," she said. "There will be a contest to find the most worthy Amazon."

"Why send one of my sisters when I am the best?" asked Diana.

"Your place is in the palace with me," Hippolyta said. "You cannot compete."

Diana put on a disguise and entered the contest anyway.

The trial of the Amazons began. There was a chariot race. An archery contest. And a sword fight!

Only one Amazon did well in each event. She left her competition in the dust.

At the end of the day, the winner
was revealed. She removed her
helmet. Everyone gasped at the sight
of Princess Diana!

Queen Hippolyta was furious. "You disobeyed me, Diana," she said. "But you have also proven yourself worthy. I must give these gifts to you."

Hippolyta opened a golden trunk. Inside was a special tiara. Next to it was a pair of unbreakable silver bracelets. And the Lasso of Truth lay on the other side.

"I will make all the Amazons proud," Diana said. "I will become a brave hero!"

On that day, Wonder Woman was born!

To travel to places outside Themyscira,
Diana uses her Invisible Jet.

This way, no one will ever find the secret location of the Amazons' island.

Diana arrives in the United States. She creates a secret identity for herself and gets a job. From there, she keeps a close eye on activities all over the world.

Suddenly, there is an increase in violence in another country. War has erupted between neighboring villages.

"Ares!" Diana says to herself. "By spreading hatred, he is fueling his own power. He must be stopped!"

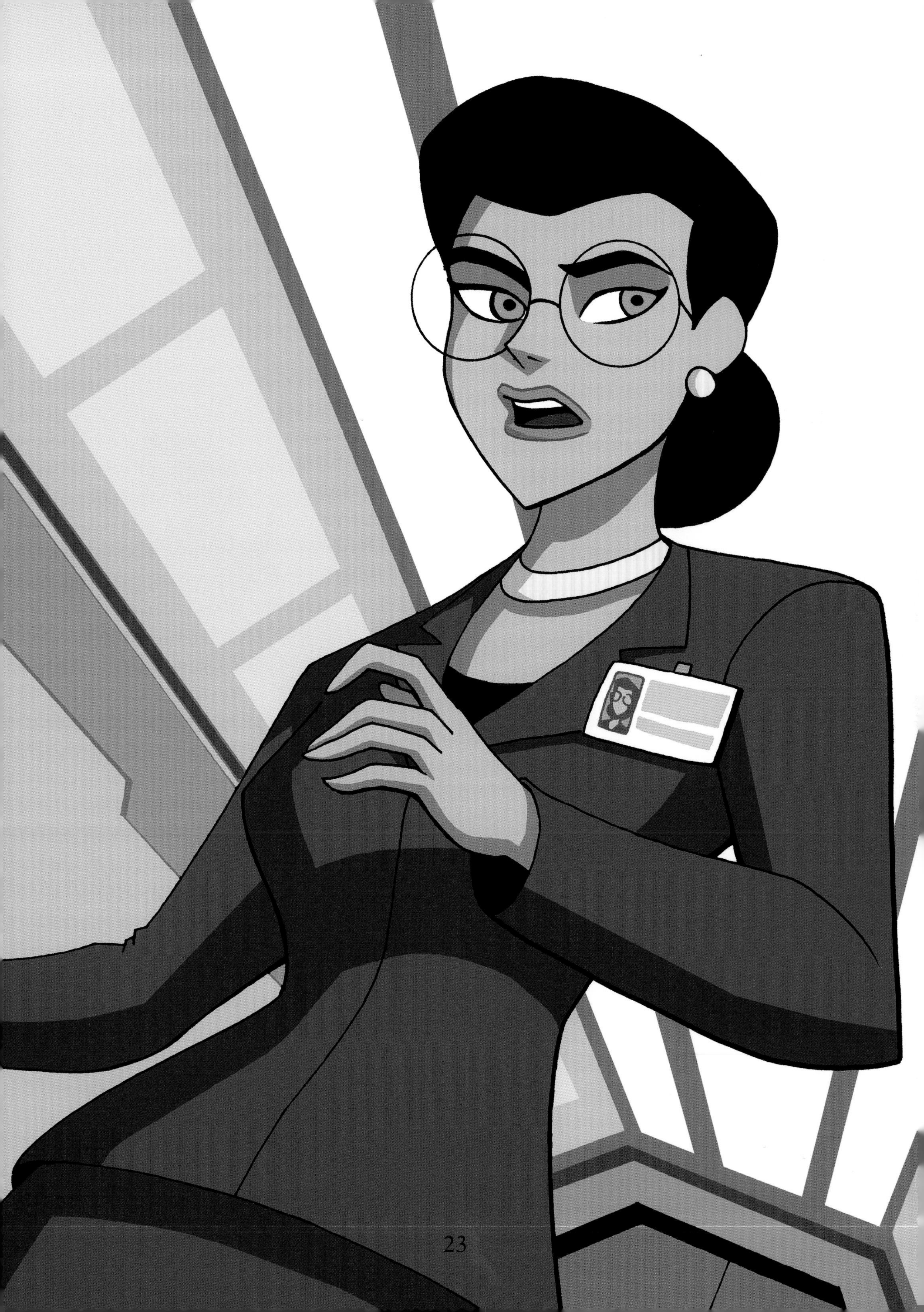

Diana sneaks into a quiet area where no one can see her. Then she twirls and twirls. She transforms into Wonder Woman!

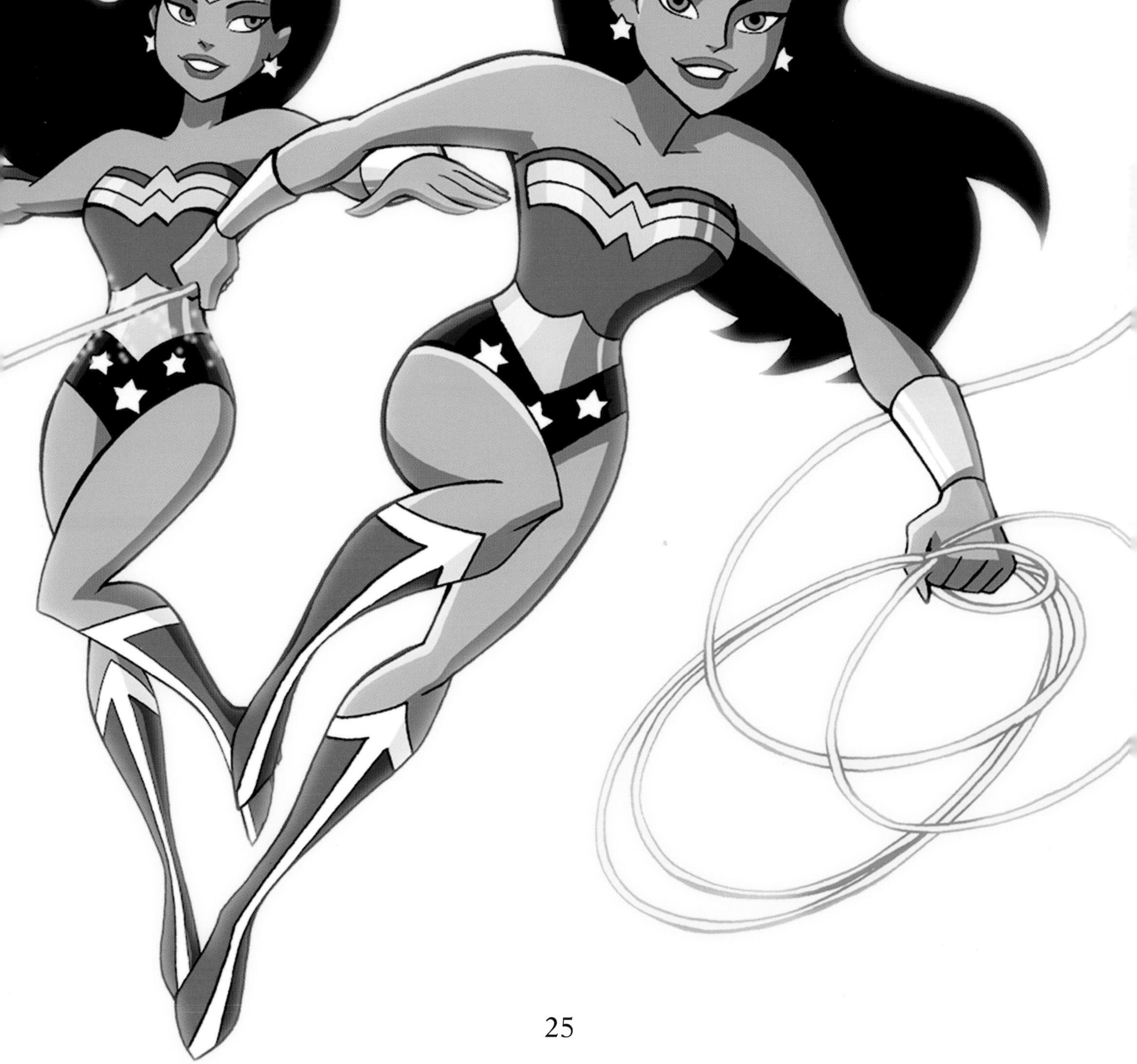

Wonder Woman flies straight into the warzone. She startles the soldiers. They turn on her and fire their weapons. The amazing Amazon blocks the blasts with her shining silver bracelets.

"My brothers," she commands. "Please see reason. Show compassion to one another."

The soldiers lay down their arms. They begin to talk. They take one step closer to understanding each other.

As the fighting fades, Ares's strength also weakens. The god of war is angry. Wonder Woman has ruined his plan.

Ares appears on the battlefield. He challenges Wonder Woman. "I will strike down anyone who stands in my way!" he cries.

The two warriors charge each other. The battle is fierce.

"Your power comes from hate," Wonder Woman says to Ares. "But my power comes from love. And that is much stronger!"

Combining her glorious gifts,
Wonder Woman banishes Ares back
to the Underworld. With the god of
war gone, peace returns.

The hero heads back home.

But more villains turn up. Some of them are BIG trouble.

Giganta can grow to the size of a building. She charges through the city! Wonder Woman puts an end to her rampage with one well-placed punch.

"The bigger they are, the harder they fall," she says.

Other foes keep Wonder Woman on her toes. Circe is an evil enchantress. She can turn people into animals. Her pets must follow her orders.

Luckily, Wonder Woman can communicate with the animals. She quickly turns the tables on the mean mistress of magic!

Cheetah is a master thief. She is robbing the First National Bank!

Wonder Woman arrives at the
scene. But Cheetah is too fast. The
feline criminal escapes!

Wonder Woman lassoes one of the henchmen. "Tell me where Cheetah is going," she says.

Caught in the Lasso of Truth, the thug cannot lie. He reveals the location of Cheetah's hideout.

Minutes later, the amazing Amazon arrives.

The feline felon is no match for Wonder Woman!

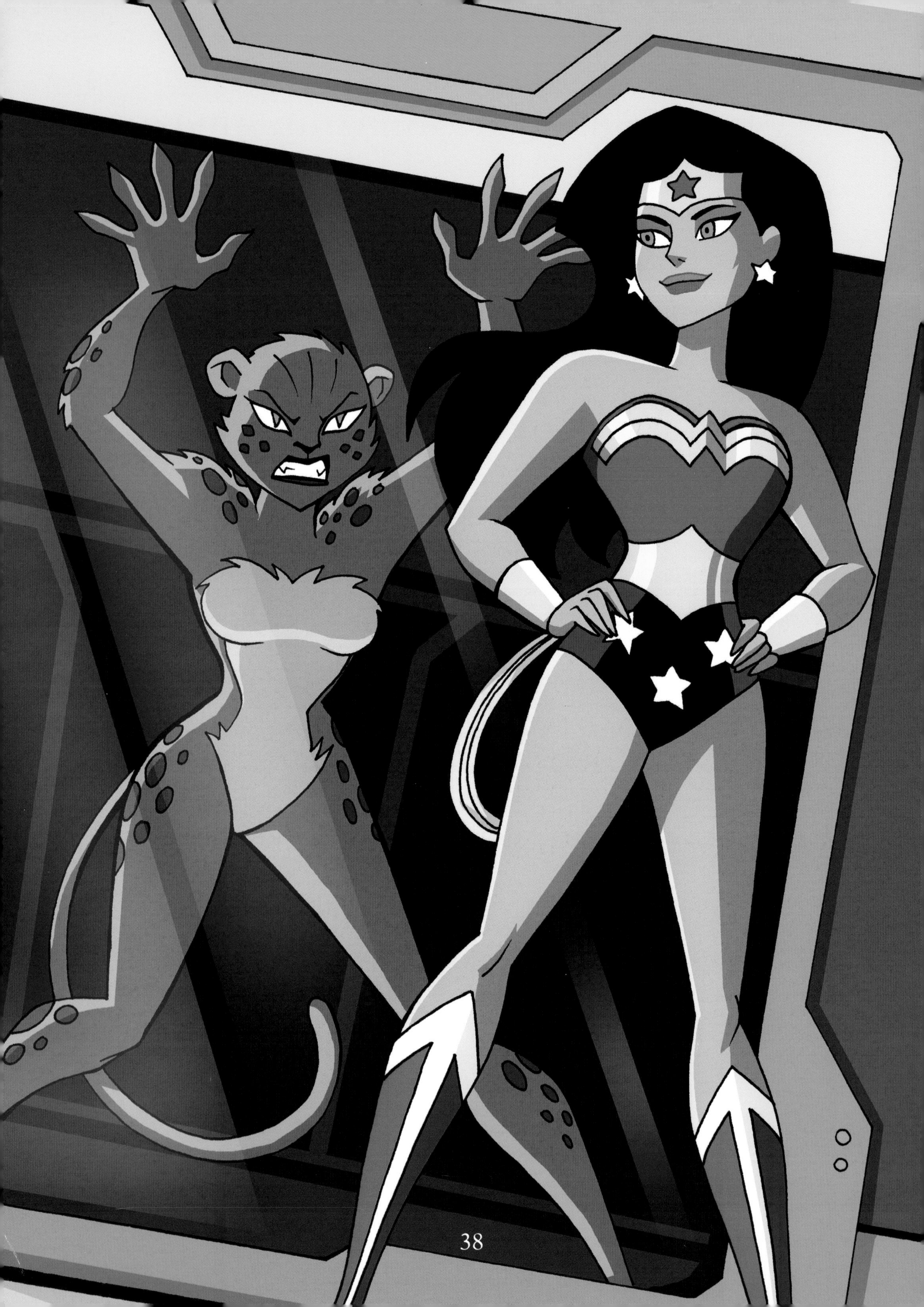

The money is returned to the bank.

"This cat belongs in a cage," Wonder Woman says.

And so Cheetah finds herself a new home — in the city jail!

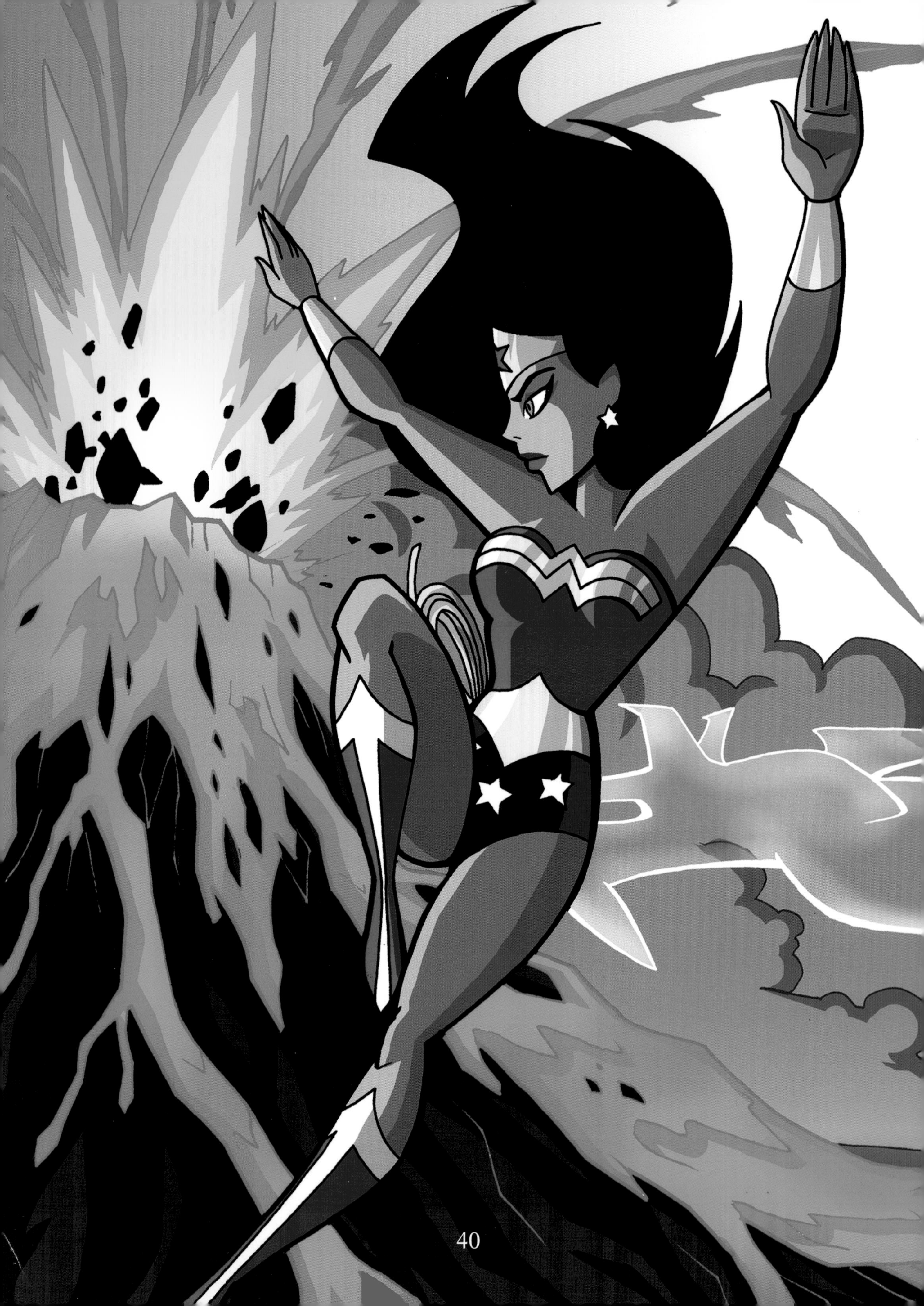

Diana of Themyscira is a princess and a warrior. But more importantly, she is a champion for peace as well as justice.

She is a super hero.

She is Wonder Woman!

WONDER WOMAN ™

REAL NAME: DIANA PRINCE

ROLE: AMAZON WARRIOR

BASE: THEMYSCIRA

As the princess of a secret island called Themyscira, Diana was fated to one day take the throne as Queen of the Amazons. Instead, she chose to become a protector of Earth: Wonder Woman!

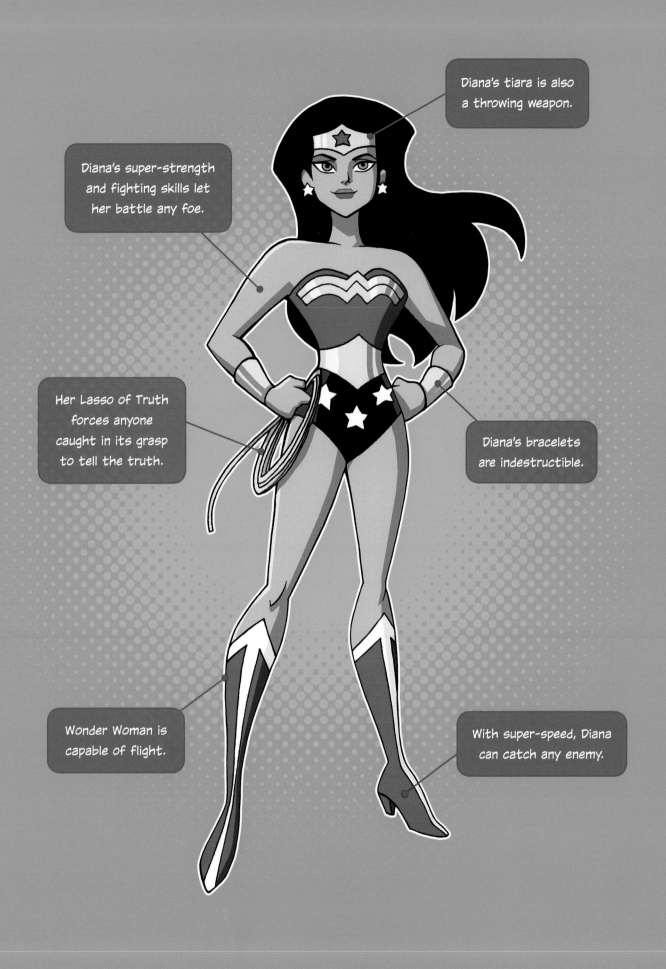

Diana's tiara is also a throwing weapon.

Diana's super-strength and fighting skills let her battle any foe.

Her Lasso of Truth forces anyone caught in its grasp to tell the truth.

Diana's bracelets are indestructible.

Wonder Woman is capable of flight.

With super-speed, Diana can catch any enemy.

THE AUTHOR

New York Times bestselling author **JOHN SAZAKLIS** enjoys writing children's books about his favorite characters. He has also illustrated Spider-Man books and created toys used in MAD Magazine. To him, it's a dream come true! John lives with his beautiful wife in New York City.

THE ILLUSTRATOR

LUCIANO VECCHIO was born in 1982 and currently lives in Buenos Aires, Argentina. With experience in illustration, animation, and comics, his works have been published in the US, Spain, UK, France, and Argentina. His credits include Ben 10 (DC Comics), Cruel Thing (Norma), Unseen Tribe (Zuda Comics), and Sentinels (Drumfish Productions).

GLOSSARY

ambassador (am-BASS-uh-der)—the highest-ranking person who represents his or her own government while living in another country

banishes (BAN-ish-iz)—forces someone to leave somewhere as a punishment

champion (CHAM-pee-uhn)—someone who fights or speaks publicly in support of a person, belief, or cause

compassion (kuhm-PASH-uhn)—a feeling of wanting to help someone who is sick, hungry, or in trouble

enchantress (en-CHAN-triss)—a woman who uses spells or magic

etiquette (ET-i-kett)—the rules indicating the proper and polite way to behave

heir (AIR)—a person who has the legal right to receive the property or titles of someone who dies

lush (LUHSH)—covered with healthy green plants or having a lot of full and healthy growth

tribe (TRAHYB)—a group of people that has the same language, customs, and beliefs

DISCUSSION QUESTIONS

Write down your answers. Refer back to the story for help.

QUESTION 1.

Wonder Woman has superpowers, but she doesn't always have to use them to solve problems. What are some ways Wonder Woman can use her mind to help others? Think up as many as you can.

QUESTION 2.

In this illustration, Wonder Woman's posture, or the way she stands, is very different from Cheetah's posture. Based on their postures, how do you think each character feels here?

QUESTION 3.

In this image, Diana transforms into Wonder Woman. In your own words, describe the transformation and how it takes place. What changes? Why are there four images of Wonder Woman here? Explain your answer.

QUESTION 4.

Wonder Woman's Invisible Jet lets her travel from place to place. In what ways would an invisible form of transportation be helpful for a super hero?

READ THEM ALL!!

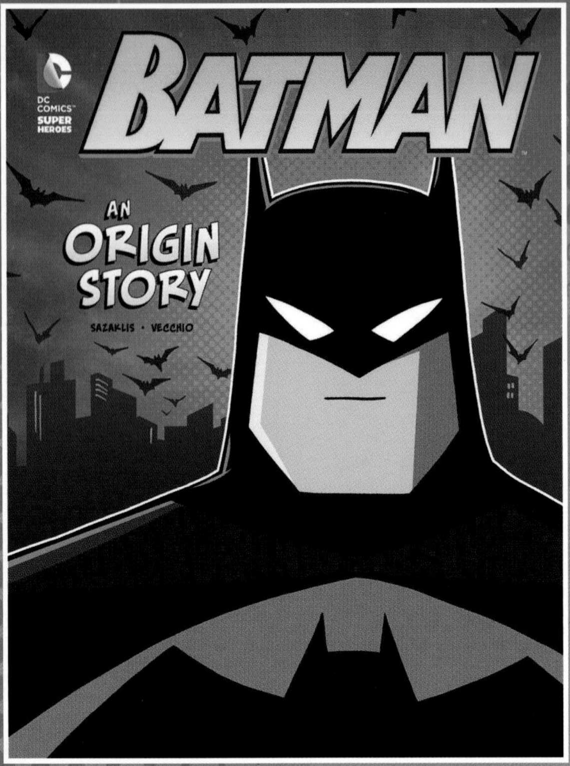
DC COMICS
SUPER HEROES
BATMAN
AN ORIGIN STORY
SAZAKLIS • VECCHIO

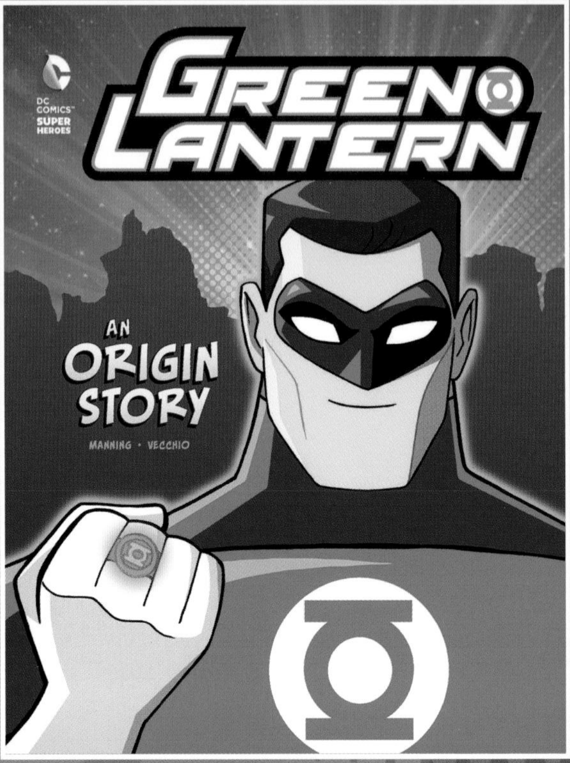
DC COMICS
SUPER HEROES
GREEN LANTERN
AN ORIGIN STORY
MANNING • VECCHIO

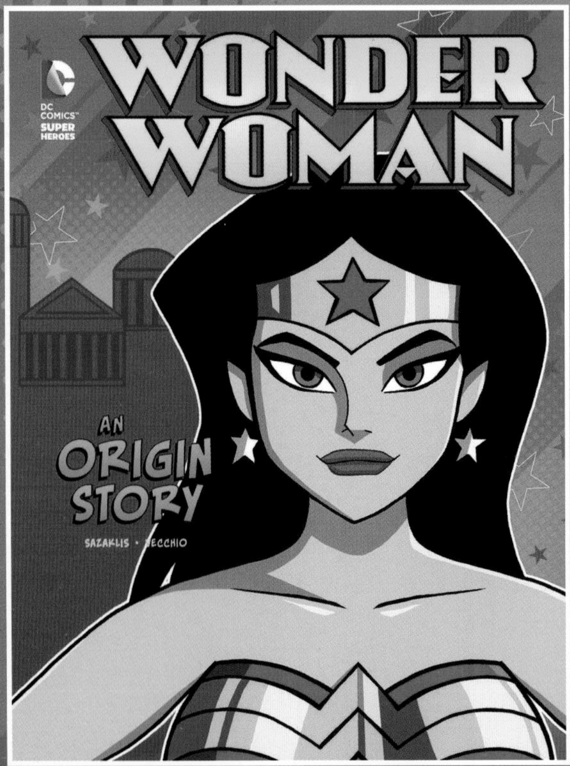
DC COMICS
SUPER HEROES
WONDER WOMAN
AN ORIGIN STORY
SAZAKLIS • VECCHIO

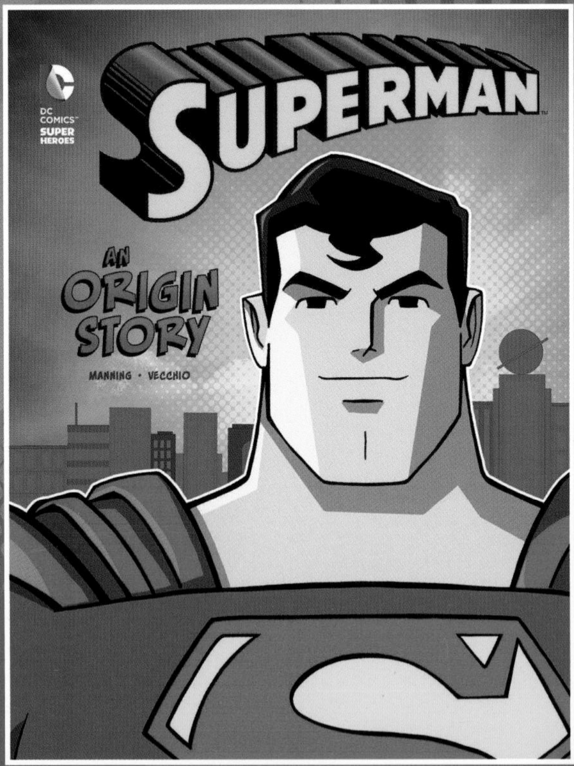
DC COMICS
SUPER HEROES
SUPERMAN
AN ORIGIN STORY
MANNING • VECCHIO